COUNTDOWN TO FLIGHT!

Other Avon Camelot Books by
Steve Englehart

CHRISTMAS COUNTDOWN
COUNTDOWN TO THE MOON
EASTER PARADE

Avon Books are available at special quantity discounts for bulk purchases for sales promotions, premiums, fund raising or educational use. Special books, or book excerpts, can also be created to fit specific needs.

For details write or telephone the office of the Director of Special Markets, Avon Books, Dept. FP, 1350 Avenue of the Americas, New York, New York 10019, 1-800-238-0658.

COUNTDOWN TO FLIGHT!

STEVE ENGLEHART

AN AVON CAMELOT BOOK

If you purchased this book without a cover, you should be aware that this book is stolen property. It was reported as "unsold and destroyed" to the publisher, and neither the author nor the publisher has received any payment for this "stripped book."

COUNTDOWN TO FLIGHT! is an original publication of Avon Books. This work has never before appeared in book form.

AVON BOOKS
A division of
The Hearst Corporation
1350 Avenue of the Americas
New York, New York 10019

Copyright © 1995 by Steve Englehart
Cover photo courtesy of Wright State University Library
All interior photos courtesy of the Library of Congress
Published by arrangement with the author
Library of Congress Catalog Card Number: 95-6193
ISBN: 0-380-77918-8
RL: 5.0

All rights reserved, which includes the right to reproduce this book or portions thereof in any form whatsoever except as provided by the U.S. Copyright Law. For information address McIntosh and Otis, Inc., 310 Madison Avenue, New York, New York 10017.

Library of Congress Cataloging in Publication Data:

Englehart, Steve.
  Countdown to flight / Steve Englehart.
    p.   cm.—(An Avon Camelot book)
Summary: A brief history of early aeronautics with a detailed account of the events leading up to the historic flight of the Wright brothers at Kitty Hawk, N.C., in 1903.
1. Flight—History—Juvenile literature. 2. Airplanes—North Carolina—Kitty Hawk—History—Juvenile literature. 3. Wright, Orville, 1871–1948—Juvenile literature. 4. Wright, Wilbur, 1867–1912—Juvenile literature. [1. Flight—History. 2. Wright, Orville, 1871–1948. 3. Wilbur, 1867–1912.] I. Title.
TL670.5.E53 1995   95-6193
629.13'09—dc20   CIP
                                                                                  AC

First Avon Camelot Printing: October 1995

CAMELOT TRADEMARK REG. U.S. PAT. OFF. AND IN OTHER COUNTRIES, MARCA REGISTRADA, HECHO EN U.S.A.

Printed in the U.S.A.

OPM 10 9 8 7 6 5 4 3 2 1

To Martha Rupel Englehart,
whose uncle also worked to find
the secrets of manned flight

With special thanks to Terry Englehart

Contents

Preface
1

The Wright Brothers
3

Five Years To Flight: 1899
13

Four Years To Flight: 1900
25

Three Years To Flight: 1901
33

Two Years To Flight: 1902
41

One Year To Flight: 1903
49

Afterword
63

COUNTDOWN TO FLIGHT!

Preface

Simon Newcomb was the leading American astronomer of the nineteenth century. He worked for the United States Naval Observatory as head of the Nautical Almanac Office, where he devised the tables used worldwide for calculating the positions of the planets. He had a vast understanding of the heavens and an open, inquiring mind.

In October 1903, Simon Newcomb published an article concluding, by "unassailable logic," that man would never create a heavier-than-air flying machine.

In December 1903, the Wright brothers did just that.

Simon Newcomb was anything but a fool. It was just that in the entire history of the world, no one had ever succeeded in that fabulous dream. . . .

The Wright Brothers

Wilbur Wright was born on April 16, 1867 on a farm near Millville, Indiana. He was the third child of Susan Koerner Wright and Milton Wright, a Protestant Minister with the United Brethren Church. A little less than three years later, Susan Wright gave birth to twins, but one died immediately and the other succumbed a month later. The Wrights' next child, born on August 19, 1871, in Dayton, Ohio, was named Orville. Though these two boys were separated by more than four years, they grew to be very much like twins themselves. "From the time we were little children, my brother Orville and myself lived together, played together, worked together, and in fact thought together," wrote Wilbur Wright in his later years.

During the boys' childhood, the family, which also included two older brothers and a younger sister, moved occasionally, as Milton Wright's duties demanded, to different parts of the Midwest. In 1878, the family relocated to Cedar Rapids, Iowa. In 1881, they moved to Richmond, Indiana. Three years later, in 1884, they went back to Dayton, this time to stay.

7 Hawthorne Street, Dayton, Ohio—the Wright family home until 1914. LC-W851-65

When Wilbur was thirteen and Orville was nine, their father returned from one of his ministerial trips with a small toy which fascinated the boys. It was a rubber band-powered *hélicoptère*, made by Alphonse Pénaud of France. The boys spent endless hours with this flying toy and were inspired to create their own versions of it. This was typical of the boys, who delighted in imagining all sorts of things and then trying to create them. When they wondered about how something worked, they would take it apart, examine it, perhaps improve it, and then put it back together. Their mother was very handy at fixing things around the house, and encouraged the boys' mechanical abilities.

Orville was a mischievous youngster who at one time was suspended from school because of his pranks. But he was very good at learning, often teaching himself a subject by going to the library and doing research. He was impulsive, energetic, and optimistic, but very shy among strangers. Once, in order to move to the next grade in elementary school, he had to read a long passage from a book to school officials. He read it perfectly—but he was holding the book upside down! In fact, he had memorized the whole passage to be certain his nervousness wouldn't cause him to slip up. In later years, after he grew famous, Orville refused all public speaking offers.

Wilbur, on the other hand, was quite articulate and would later handle public presentations admirably. Like his brother, he preferred to live inside his head, and rarely volunteered anything, but he did what he had to do to make his point. When Wilbur was in elementary school, he did an arithmetic problem which his teacher graded as wrong. Another student was assigned to help him find the correct answer. By the time they were done, Wilbur had not only convinced the other student, but even the teacher, that he'd been right all along.

Wilbur planned to attend divinity school at Yale University after his graduation from high school, and was a fine athlete, excelling at running. But in 1885, when he was eighteen, he was accidentally struck hard in the face during an ice-skating game. The injury itself seems to have been minor, but it caused a shock to Wilbur's system which led to heart palpitations and problems with his digestion.

A period of extended rest was prescribed, and indeed, it was nearly two years before the doctor pronounced Wilbur cured. But the sudden infirmities, the long recuperation, and the loss of a chance to get out in the world, right when he was ready to take it, left the young man feeling like a "potential invalid." He began to think that living a normal life might be beyond him, and he slipped into a depression that lasted another year. Between 1885 and 1888 he lived almost entirely inside the Wright house, reading. Fortunately, the Wright family valued education, so his reading consisted of encyclopedias, history, and biography.

During that time, his mother, whose health had also been uncertain throughout her life, developed tuberculosis. Wilbur lovingly cared for her despite his depression. Possibly this dedication to someone who was a true invalid showed him that he still could live his own life. In any event, Wilbur pulled himself out of his depression through a reborn force of will. Though he had abandoned his idea of studying for the ministry, he joined in his father's church work, even as he continued to care for his failing mother.

In 1889, Susan Koerner Wright died. Bishop Wright still needed to travel frequently for his church, so the family's one daughter, Katharine, took on the duties of running the household at age fifteen. Unlike many men of the time, Bishop Wright believed absolutely in the equality of men and women, so Katharine received the same excellent education as her brothers, and in fact became the only one of the three to graduate from college. But like most men and women of the time, Bishop Wright and Katharine believed that her career was in the home. Still, she would always be close to the intellectual pursuits of the two brothers who preceded her in the family. Through the years she was a wonderful support to Wilbur and Orville, encouraging them in their creative endeavors and becoming their lifelong confidante.

Meanwhile, Orville had developed an interest in printing. When the family came back to Dayton in 1884, he found that a friend from his earlier time in the city had a small printing press. The following year, the two boys started a newspaper for their school class called *The Midget*. As they got more and more caught up in printing, Wilbur and another brother, Lorin, gave them a better press, while Bishop Wright gave them better type. Orville worked as a summer apprentice in a local print shop for two years and seemed destined for printing as a career. As his friend began to lose interest, Orville moved the operation into the Wright home, tirelessly researching what he did not know and creating new devices as he needed them. In 1888, he decided to tackle the bigger job of building his own press and asked Wilbur, who was just coming out of his seclusion, to help. Wilbur did join in, and soon a new print shop appeared in Dayton: "Wright Bros."

In truth, Wilbur was still more interested in his father's work than his brother's. But in 1889, the brothers launched a professional weekly newspaper, *The West Side News,* with Wilbur as the editor. The two brothers relearned what they'd known as children, that they worked well together, with wonderful rapport, despite the difference in their ages (which, as time went on, became less important). A year later, *The West Side News* became a daily paper, named *The Evening Item.* But competition in the Dayton newspaper market was fierce, and the daily paper lasted only four months. The brothers went back to job printing.

In 1892, the printing business had slowed down so much that the brothers' agile minds were becoming bored. They developed an interest in the bicycle craze which was sweeping America. Bicycles had first been invented in 1878, with one large wheel and one small one. The "safety" bicycle, with two wheels of equal size, was developed in 1887, and five years later, everybody wanted one. Wilbur and Orville started out bicycling for pleasure, but, as always, they didn't just make use of the machines, they taught themselves to understand and repair them. Once they'd done that, they decided to open a bicycle sales shop as a second business. The shop expanded rapidly, eclipsing the print shop, and Wilbur and Orville were soon designing and building their own bicycles. Their bicycle operation generated real money for the first time in the boys' lives. Certainly, they had found their life's work at last.

But late in August 1896, Orville was stricken with typhoid. The fever overwhelmed him quickly. Within a week he was continually delirious. Wilbur and Katharine sat by his bedside, feeding him, bathing him, and reading to him to let him know they were there. Wilbur, scanning the newspaper one day, happened upon a small news item, reporting that Otto Lilienthal was dead.

The brothers had first heard of the German engineer and his experiments with flying gliders back in 1890, when they ran a story about him in *The Evening Item*. In 1894, they'd read a magazine article about his work. Now he was dead, the victim of a glider accident. In the days that followed, Wilbur sat by Orville's bedside, with plenty of time to think about the worldwide search for a flying machine. As a successful mechanic, he became intrigued, remembering the *hélicoptère* . . .

Orville's fever finally broke in early October, but he remained bedridden a while longer. In that time, Wilbur explained what he'd had on his mind, and Orville soon joined in the discussion. Both of them were fascinated by this possible new challenge, but both of them were still too caught up in their long-awaited business success at the bicycle shop to do anything further. When Orville was fully recovered, they put ideas of

Wilbur and Orville Wright on the back porch of their home in Dayton, Ohio.   LC-USZ62-65478

"aeroplanes" on the back burner and went back to two-wheelers.

Still, they kept their eyes on the news, as the century played itself out and no one met the challenge.

Five Years To Flight: 1899

On June 2, 1899, Richard Rathbun, assistant secretary of the Smithsonian Institution in Washington, D.C., received a letter from Dayton, Ohio. The letter read in part:

I have been interested in the problem of mechanical and human flight ever since as a boy I constructed a number of bats of various sizes after the style of Cayley's and Pénaud's machines.... I believe that simple flight at least is possible to man and that the experiments and investigations of a large number of independent workers will result in the accumulation of information and knowledge and skill which will finally lead to accomplished flight.... I am about to begin a systematic study of the subject in preparation for practical work to which I expect to devote what time I can spare from my regular business. I wish to obtain such papers as the

Smithsonian Institution has published on this subject, and if possible a list of other works in print in the English language. I am an enthusiast, but not a crank in the sense that I have some pet theories as to the proper construction of a flying machine. I wish to avail myself of all that is already known and then if possible add my mite to help on the future worker who will attain final success. I do not know the terms on which you send out your publications but if you will inform me of the cost I will remit the price.

It was signed by Wilbur Wright, of the Wright Cycle Company. The most interesting thing about it, in retrospect, is that Orville is nowhere mentioned. Clearly, for the first time in their association, Wilbur, the "potential invalid," was taking the lead on a project. After 32 years of going nowhere, he felt that he needed a serious challenge, to see what he was really made of.

As experimentation on flying machines had picked up in the late 1890's, the Smithsonian had been besieged by letters from inventors hoping to build the first one. They had a standard package of several pamphlets and a list of further reading material, which they sent to everyone, including Wilbur. He and his brother studied everything he received with great eagerness, and plundered the local library for anything else they could find. Some of it was inspirational, but the rest was fruitless speculation. And much of what passed for "fact" was simply wrong. Said Wilbur, "Thousands of men had thought about flying machines and a few had even built machines which they called flying machines, but these were guilty of almost everything except *flying*." Wilbur and Orville would find in the next few years that they would have to disregard most of what they had read and start from scratch, but here is what they did read at the end of the nineteenth century.

Humans had always marveled at the unrestrained soaring of birds and envied them their freedom from the heavy pull of Earth's gravity. But most humans never imagined that they would join them in the air, certain that if humans were meant to fly, they would have been born with wings.

Many ancient legends tell of angels, devils, winged animals, and flying carpets. A Greek myth tells of Daedalus and his son Icarus, who tried to escape imprisonment by flying with wings they had made of feathers and wax. According to the story, Daedalus made it to safety, but Icarus flew too close to the sun, his wax melted, his wings fell apart and he plummeted into the sea.

Over 2500 years ago, the Chinese made small propeller-driven toys which could fly straight up into the air. There is even evidence that kites were flown in China as early as 200 or 300 B.C.

An English monk of the thirteenth century,

Roger Bacon, wrote about "ornithopters," which, he imagined, would fly by the flapping of wings.

An Italian monk of the seventeenth century was said to be able to fly on his own, through spiritual powers. His name was Joseph of Cupertino, and the Catholic Church was certain enough of his ability that in the next century it made him a saint.

During the "Renaissance" of the fourteenth century, Leonardo da Vinci of Italy drew up a number of plans for flying machines, even though there were no engines at the time that could supply the power to fly and people were not strong enough to provide the power themselves. Da Vinci's ideas were not published until 1797, so few knew of his research. If the information had been circulated earlier, flight experimentation might well have moved ahead more quickly.

Those who did experiment usually came to a bad end. A number of what have been called "tower jumpers" tried to fly by attaching wings to their bodies and jumping off high places. Oliver of Malmesbury, an English monk of the eleventh century, broke his legs after leaping from a wall to the ground far below. Giovanni Danti of Italy tried to glide from a tower in 1490 and was badly hurt when he fell straight down instead. The Marquis de Bocqueville of Paris was injured when, in 1742, he jumped off a high building on the bank of the River Seine in an attempt to fly across, and plunged to a barge below.

It was not until 1783 that the Montgolfier brothers of France safely flew a hot air balloon to a height of nearly 6,000 feet, and stayed in the air for ten minutes. Though they had no control of their flight direction, they landed with no problem.

The first success in the field of winged flight came from Sir George Cayley, mentioned in Wilbur's letter above. Cayley was an Englishman who, in 1804, built the first glider that could actually fly, and, in 1853, the first glider that carried a man. Cayley believed that although birds flapped their wings in flight, a fixed wing would work better for man. It was Cayley who discovered that lift, the upward force opposing gravity, could be created by use of a wing curved on top, and that by increasing the size of the wing and the speed of air flowing over its surface, lift could be increased. This works because air passes more quickly over the curved part of a wing than under its flat bottom, and the faster moving air creates a lower pressure area. The higher pressure beneath the wing then pushes it upward.

Two other English inventors, William Henson and John Stringfellow, were, in 1844, the first to build a large model of a fixed-wing flying machine with propellers. The model failed to fly for the first four years of its existence, but in 1848 Stringfellow built a smaller, lighter model which did fly about 120 feet. He then gave up aviation work until 1868, when he built a model of a triplane—a plane with three wings stacked one above the other—to display at the first Aeronautical Exhibition in London.

Otto Lilienthal made over 2,000 glider flights

before an unexpected gust of wind killed him in 1896, and his flights developed the first real body of knowledge concerning mid-air equilibrium. Lilienthal used a wing with a slight bulge on the top front of the wing, curving gently toward the back. He had seen just such a curve in his thorough studies of birds and was convinced this was the secret to lifting power. To control his glider, he relied upon a shift of body weight to move the center of gravity and keep in balance. He also thought that to maintain flight it would be necessary to flap the wings, but he died before he was able to put this last idea into practice.

Octave Chanute, born in France but raised in the United States, designed a number of gliders in the 1890s which he hired others, including a

Otto Lilienthal preparing to fly with his glider. LC-USZ62-19649

young man named Augustus Herring, to build for him. He also hired young men to fly the resulting gliders, as he was in his sixties at the time and felt that he could not meet the physical demands of flying. Chanute had corresponded with experimenters from around the world and had collected a great deal of information about aeronautical research, which he published in *Progress in Flying Machines* in 1894, a book the Wright brothers devoured.

Lawrence Hargrave of Australia developed the box kite in 1893. This kite was not intended as a toy but rather a means of researching aircraft wings. It was also used by the United States Weather Bureau to check barometric pressure at high altitudes.

Samuel Langley, secretary of the Smithsonian Institution and a well known scientist, built scale model flying machines, or "aerodromes," as he called them, and launched them over water in 1896. Though there was no way to control them, they flew well. A few years later, at a cost of $50,000 to the U.S. government, he built a full-sized aerodrome but was not successful in his attempts to fly it.

Wilbur might have wondered if he had the stuff to meet a real challenge, but one thing he and his brother definitely had were minds that could stay focused. As they, beginners, read through the writings of men who had devoted most if not all of their lives to the subject of flight, they were able to home in on the basic problems which had to be solved, and sift through the speculation for

Those Who Dared

There were many others who had attempted sustained flight in a machine but failed. Felix Du Temple, a Frenchman, in 1874 designed a hot air–powered vehicle with one wing, a tail in the back, a propeller in the front, and three wheels for landing. It made a short hop, but did not fly.

Alexander Mozhaiski, a Russian, attempted to fly a huge, heavy machine in 1884. This one hopped and then crashed.

In 1894, Hiram Maxim, an American, built an even bigger machine which he called a "steam kite." This enormous four-ton flying machine, with a wingspan of over 100 feet, also turned out to be incapable of flight.

In 1897, Clément Ader, a French engineer backed by the French War Department, made false claims of successful flights with his bat-like crafts, but was soon exposed.

The first rigid airship was built by an Austrian, David Schwartz, in 1897. This ambitious machine was made of aluminum and was to be driven by two propellers powered by a 12-horsepower gasoline engine. But the craft didn't fly and wrecked on its first attempt.

answers. They quickly determined that there were really only three such problems:

1. Wings needed to lift an aeroplane into the air.
2. An engine had to move it once it was in the air.

3. They needed a way to control the movement of the craft.

It seemed to them that the men who had gone before them had done most of the work on the wings and the engine. And as the Wright brothers progressed on their own work, they would be able to draw on what Lilienthal, Chanute, and Langley had already done. The big question was control, and that was where they expected to spend most of their energies.

(Later, the brothers would realize that each flying machine was the sum of many different design ideas, so that work on one machine rarely translated directly to another. That meant problems 1 and 2 would have to be solved after all, and more than once. But this is where they began.)

Now the close relationship between the minds of the Wright brothers came into play. As Wilbur started working through the various theories of flight control, he began to bounce his ideas off his brother—and Orville, for his part, began to match his interest in the quest. They spent countless hours discussing the problems before them and arguing about possible solutions. Though they were very different, their minds worked in wonderful synchronicity, challenging one another constantly. Often they would both be so successful in arguing a point that they would switch sides and begin to argue against their previously held ideas.

In the systematic experiments they undertook,

they were very observant and they kept careful records of all the data gathered. Each experiment led directly to the next; they refused to gain results through trial and error. This methodical approach was a major difference between the brothers and the other experimenters of their day.

First, they had to figure out how to control the balance on their aircraft so it wouldn't tip over and crash in a sudden gust of wind, as had happened to Lilienthal. To balance the wing lift, they decided to put a smaller flat horizontal surface, which could be raised or lowered, in front of the wings. They called it a "horizontal rudder," or elevator, and its purpose was to control the pressure of air moving along the wings, maintaining front-to-back equilibrium. All of the early Wright brothers' planes had this feature, which saved their lives many times by preventing a nosedive and allowing the aircraft to "parachute" to the ground without spinning out.

But there was also the problem of side-to-side equilibrium. Lilienthal had thought the answer was shifting the pilot's center of gravity to one side or the other, but Wilbur's observations of birds showed him that they didn't operate that way. Watching a pigeon fly, he devised the idea of "wingwarping," in which the wingtips could be manipulated or twisted, one up and one down, to counterbalance any change in the air. The question was, how could that idea be applied to a mechanical object? Wilbur hit upon an idea in the bicycle shop one day, as he idly twisted the ends of a long, empty inner tube box back and forth.

While Orville tended to the daily bicycle business, Wilbur designed and built a kite which would test his new theory. The kite's wingspan was five feet and the wing's front-to-back measurement was 13 inches. This kite was a biplane (one wing on top of another), with six struts of bamboo connecting the top and bottom wings, and wires crisscrossing from the leading edge of one wing to the trailing edge of the other wing. He flew the kite on July 27, 1899, manipulating the wingtips by pulling at several lines, and was thrilled at the control and balance that was achieved.

The 1900 glider being flown as a kite to test its stability.   LC-W851-96

The bicycle business was seasonal. As the colder weather came in the fall, the brothers had less and less to do in running their shop, and more and more time to experiment. They began planning to build a full-sized glider that would carry a man. They knew there was great risk to the life of the pilot, but they hoped to minimize this risk by studying the subject completely, testing materials, compiling data, and going ahead as slowly as was necessary to be thorough and intelligent in the process. On October 2, in the midst of their work, they were reminded just how dangerous it could be by the death of Percy Pilcher, a Scottish experimenter. He had followed Lilienthal's procedures, relying on his body weight to achieve stability, and had crashed to earth the same way.

In November of 1899, they began their search for a test site, writing to the Weather Bureau and anyone else who might have helpful information, looking for a place with steady winds and a relatively safe, smooth, treeless surface. They were ready to take their next step.

Four Years To Flight: 1900

On May 13, 1900, Wilbur began correspondence with Octave Chanute. He wrote:

For some years I have been afflicted with the belief that flight is possible to man. My disease has increased in severity and I feel that it will soon cost me an increased amount of money if not my life. I have been trying to arrange my affairs in such a way that I can devote my entire time for a few months to experiment in this field. It is possible to fly without motors, but not without knowledge and skill. This I conceive to be fortunate, for man, by reason of his greater intellect, can more reasonably hope to equal birds in knowledge, than to equal nature in the perfection of her machinery.

He then went on to ask for advice on several points, including a place for test flights.

Chanute, like Wilbur, believed that progress in flight would come from many people working on the problem, so he was happy to assist the younger man. He wrote back that he "preferred preliminary learning on a sand hill and trying ambitious feats over water," suggesting a spot "on the Atlantic coast."

Going through the information he'd received from the Weather Bureau, Wilbur found that the five best places for constant wind in America were too built up for test flights. But the sixth was an isolated spot named Kitty Hawk, on the Outer Banks of North Carolina, an area separated from the mainland by a forty-mile-wide sound. That seemed good, so he wrote to the Weather Bureau office in Kitty Hawk, and was reassured that the wind was steady and the sand might help cushion a hard landing. In addition, there were no tall trees or other obstructions.

Wilbur and Orville prepared the parts for their first glider in their Dayton bicycle shop, then packed them up for the long journey to North Carolina. Into a large trunk went the sections of the plane, the tools for assembling it, and yards and yards of white sateen fabric which had been sewn to cover the wings. To be purchased later in Norfolk, Virginia, the last big town they'd pass through on the journey to Kitty Hawk, were the long pieces of wood for the front and back edges of the wings. The cost of the glider's materials would total all of $15.

Wilbur left by train on September 6, while Orville stayed behind to mind the store. Orville was to join him on September 28, after the bicycle season slowed down enough that someone else could look after the business.

It took Wilbur seven days to get to Kitty Hawk, four of which were spent in Elizabeth City, North Carolina, just trying to find a boat to take him the rest of the way. The only one he could arrange for was in poor condition, and Wilbur spent a harrowing night and day on the long, windy voyage. He was quite relieved when he finally set foot on the Kitty Hawk dock.

While waiting for his brother, Wilbur worked hard putting the glider together. The only wood he had been able to buy in Virginia was two feet shorter than the 18-foot wingspan they had designed, so the carefully-measured fabric covering had to be resewn and adjusted. Fortunately, the people of Kitty Hawk were very hospitable. Mr. and Mrs. William Tate, who ran the post office, offered him a room in their home, and the use of Mrs. Tate's sewing machine. When Orville arrived on the twenty-eighth, he shared Wilbur's room until they set up a large tent on October 4. Bill Tate brought them dishes, a gasoline stove, and a barrel of gasoline after a buying trip to Elizabeth City. The Tates also occasionally invited them to dinner.

The Wright brothers were, in their clean collars, neckties, and hats, an unusual sight in Kitty Hawk. Wilbur was about 5 feet 10 inches tall, and weighed close to 140 pounds. He was nearly bald in early adulthood and had blue-gray eyes with gold flecks. Orville, a little heavier and shorter than Wilbur, was considered handsome with a moustache and a bit more hair than his brother. Orville had a sense of style and liked to wear the latest fashions, while Wilbur was not as concerned with his appearance.

Their letters to their sister and their father, as well as Wilbur's detailed notes, have given us a wonderful record of their experiences. The letters were usually written on Sunday, because the brothers had promised their father they would not work on the Sabbath. The brothers also took excellent photographs to record their progress.

Milton Wright was understandably concerned, reading about the dangers facing his sons in their flight experiments. To reassure his father, early on that first trip to Kitty Hawk, Wilbur wrote, "In my experiments I do not expect to rise many feet from the ground, and in case I am upset there is nothing but soft sand to strike on. I do not intend to take dangerous chances, both because I do not wish to get hurt and because a fall would stop my experimenting, which I would not like at all."

On the first day of their tests, they began by flying the 50-pound glider like a kite, testing the controls by using long strings. Soon, however, Wilbur just had to take a ride. Orville and Bill Tate held the wings until the wind picked the glider off the sand, then Wilbur shinnied on top. Swiftly, he rose 15 feet in the air—then the craft began to buck. Wilbur immediately called to be brought down, though Orville protested that he ought to have kept going. But Wilbur said, "I promised Pop I'd take care of myself."

The next day the wind was very light so it could not support a man. That day Tom Tate, Bill Tate's young nephew, hung on a few times to provide ballast. Other times chains were used, since most of the time the two brothers worked by themselves. One week after they began, their glider was left unattended for a moment, and was badly broken up by a sudden gust of wind. They had to spend three days rebuilding it.

The Wright brothers performed many tests over the following weeks, and, since this was their first time out with their new design, they encountered many problems. These had to do with the angle at which the wing must hit the air, the necessary square footage of wing surface, the amount of curvature of the wing, the weight the glider could carry at a safe wind speed, and how to handle a stall when the lifting power would suddenly be gone.

Up to that point they had used wings which were slightly higher at the tips than where they met the glider's body, forming a broad V when seen from front or back. But they learned from these experiments that straight wings were better. This gave them better control when hit from the side by a gust of wind. Their wingwarping experiments also went well, adding to their side-to-side balance as they made their long, straight glides.

They were baffled for weeks by the rapidly changing center of air pressure beneath the wings. With a flat wing, the center of pressure moves forward as its angle to the wind is decreased. When the wing becomes horizontal and is parallel to the flow of air, the center of pressure is right on the front, or leading, edge. However, with a curved wing—necessary for flight, as Cayley had shown—the center of pressure moves forward as the wing angle decreases until it reaches a critical point, at which time it switches and starts moving backwards. When this happens the center of pressure causes lift behind the center of gravity and the aircraft dives. It wasn't until the brothers worked out the correct size and shape for the wings' horizontal rudders that they could counterbalance this changing center of pressure on the wings. But once they did, they had the front-to-back stability they needed. The forward position of these rudders also enabled the pilot to better see what the glider's position was in relation to the horizon.

Another achievement of the trials in 1900 was making the wind resistance of their craft lower than any other glider's had been. This was partly due to the prone position of the pilot, a change from the sitting position of previous experimenters.

Before leaving Kitty Hawk on October 23, Wilbur went back into the air to make a series of glides from the largest dune, Big Kill Devil Hill, four miles south of their camp. Bill Tate went along to help Orville steady the wings and run into the wind along with the glider. Some lift was achieved, and Wilbur was able to glide and land with no damage to himself or to the glider.

The brothers were delighted with their successes and, although they had a tremendous amount of work yet to do, they knew they would return the following year to continue their adventure. They gave the glider to Bill Tate to recycle the materials as he chose. Mrs. Tate used the white sateen fabric covering the wings to make dresses for her daughters.

Back in Dayton the Wrights analyzed their experiments and spent most of their spare time trying to figure out how to approach the remaining design problems before returning to Kitty Hawk in 1901. They often included their sister, Katharine, and their older brother, Lorin, in their discussions.

Wilbur continued his correspondence with Octave Chanute, detailing their successes and their problems. Chanute was impressed with their progress and, since he believed all advances in the field should be shared, he requested permission to write about it in an article he was preparing for a magazine. It turned out that the brothers were reluctant to agree. Wilbur, always reticent, wrote back that "it is not our intention to make a close secret of our machine, but at the same time, inasmuch as we have not yet had opportunity to test the full possibilities of our methods, we wish to be the first to give them such a test."

In the end, Chanute's article spoke only of the pilot's using a prone position.

Three Years To Flight: 1901

It was necessary for Orville and Wilbur to continue to earn an income from their bicycle shop, but most of their energy was put into their attempt to fly. In the winter and spring of 1901, they took care of their business and made plans for Lorin and Katharine to manage it while they were in North Carolina that fall. Then in June, they hired a friend, Charles Taylor, to handle the day-to-day business of the bicycle shop, and another man to help with repairs. They would be able to go back much earlier than they'd planned.

On June 26, just a week and a half before Orville and Wilbur were to return to Kitty Hawk, they were visited in Dayton by Chanute. It was a friendly social visit as well as one full of animated discussions about the possibilities of human flight. At their request, Chanute brought them an anemometer, an instrument used to measure wind velocity. For his part, the elderly Chanute asked the brothers if they would help test a glider he was building. He wanted to go to Kitty Hawk along with two of his assistants and work alongside the Wrights. Orville and Wilbur politely declined the idea of collaboration, but they later reluctantly agreed to have Chanute and his men visit Kitty Hawk, with one of the men, George Spratt, assisting the Wrights in their tests.

In early July, two short articles written by Wilbur were published in aeronautical magazines, giving him his first recognition as a researcher in aviation. Only one article even bothered to mention that he'd actually flown.

On July 7, Wilbur and Orville left for Kitty Hawk, having shipped most of their supplies, tools, and glider materials ahead of them. They planned to build a large workshed at Kill Devil Hills and live comfortably in a well-supplied camp. They arrived on July 12 in the middle of a terrible storm, and were unable to get to work building the shed for several days.

Once under way, they worked hard on their new building, whose 16-foot by 25-foot area would give them plenty of room to work. The roof, seven feet high at the sides and peaked in the middle, was covered with tar paper, and the walls were made of pine planks. The ends of the shed were hinged and could be lifted up to allow light and air to enter, and to provide easy access for the glider.

On July 18, just as they were finishing their shed, Edward Huffaker arrived with Chanute's glider. Also arriving that day were billions of mosquitoes which had hatched after the heavy rains. George Spratt arrived on July 25. Wilbur and Orville found Huffaker and the mosquitoes quite unpleasant, but they both enjoyed the company of Spratt.

On July 26, the glider was ready to fly. There were a number of differences from the 1900 glider. The wingspan was 22 feet instead of 16, and the measurement from the front of the wing to the back was seven feet instead of five. The surface area of the wings was about 308 square feet, much bigger than the previous 165. The wing curve was increased to a level Lilienthal had proposed, and the wing's leading edge was made blunter. The pilot could operate the wing-warping controls with his feet and the front elevator with his hands. The glider weighed 98 pounds, nearly double that of the previous year. Skids, similar to skis, were attached to protect the machine in landing.

On July 27, the Wrights, Spratt, Huffaker, Bill Tate, and his half-brother Dan Tate carried the glider up Big Kill Devil Hill. It was here that Wilbur climbed in for the first tests of the summer. There were several unsuccessful launches that morning, and everyone became quite frustrated. Finally the glider did fly 315 feet for 19 seconds just slightly above the ground, but only because Wilbur had fully deflected the forward elevator. The center-of-pressure problem was still giving them difficulties, and until it was solved for this new configuration, no real flight would occur.

In the next several glides, the machine did get into the air but proceeded to stall. This happened

With Wilbur as the pilot, the 1901 glider is launched by Dan Tate and Edward Huffaker. LC-W851-125

when the glider slowed down and the wing angle was increased to compensate, thereby maintaining lift. At a certain critical point when the angle was very steep, the air moving over the top broke and lift was lost. Though they hadn't yet learned to fly, the brothers did learn to greatly minimize their chances of dying while trying to fly when the forward horizontal elevator allowed the craft to settle gently to the ground.

Orville and Wilbur tackled the center-of-pressure problem by carefully observing the reactions of the upper wing when it was detached and flown as a kite in winds of various strengths. To solve the problem, they reduced the curve of the wings again. They also altered the shape of the wings' leading edge to lower their wind resistance. Thereafter, their glides became more successful.

From August 4 through 11, Octave Chanute visited the site and, though genuinely pleased at the Wrights' achievements, was disappointed in the failure of his own experiments.

On August 9, Wilbur was ready to try to turn the glider in flight for the first time, by using his wingwarping controls. He attempted to turn to the left by warping and therefore raising the right wing. But when he changed the wing's shape he created "drag," or resistance, thus slowing the right wing. The left wing moved forward even though it was lower than the right wing, so the glider began to slip sideways and control was lost. Wilbur ended up with bruises and a black eye.

Several days later more glides were made, but the unexpected problem of drag confounded and discouraged the brothers. Wilbur later wrote,

Wilbur has just landed the 1901 glider. LC-W851-111

When we left Kitty Hawk [on August 20] 1901, we doubted that we would ever resume our experiments. Although we had broken the record for distance in gliding, and although Mr. Chanute, who was present at that time, assured us that our results were better than had ever before been attained, yet when we looked at the time and money which we had expended, and considered the progress made and the distance yet to go, we considered our experiments a failure. At this time I made the prediction that man would sometime fly but that it would not be within our lifetime.

Back in Dayton, correspondence continued with Chanute, who praised the brothers' accomplishments and urged them not to give up their dream. He invited Wilbur to present a paper on their glider experiments to the distinguished Western Society of Engineers, in September in Chicago. Wilbur was naturally reluctant, but agreed after much encouragement from Katharine, who felt that the recognition would re-energize her brothers. Wilbur had no appropriate clothes to wear to the gathering so he borrowed a fashionable outfit from Orville. In the end, the presentation was very well received, and the information given was highly regarded among engineering and aeronautical professionals. Wilbur recovered his resolve.

He and Orville realized they had to throw out all of the mathematical tables and theories of curving the wing which had been put forward by previous experimenters—in effect, they had to solve problems that they had thought they would not be bothered with. In a strange way, this invigorated them, because they finally realized where their problems now lay. They had to devise a method of testing wings to determine the length-to-width ratio, the right curve, the shape of the front edge, the correct angle of exposure to the airstream, the center of pressure, and any other factors that would be significant.

Their first wing testing machine used a bicycle wheel placed horizontally on a bar on the front of another bike. The bike was then pedaled, rotating the horizontal wheel, thereby creating a fairly constant wind. This method was not as accurate as they needed so they had to think of something else.

By November 1901, the Wrights had designed a wind tunnel which could test various airfoils, or wing models, of any conceivable configuration. The tunnel was just 6 feet long and 16 inches square, and a small internal combustion engine drove the fan. All tests were done with extreme care, so any calculations were as accurate as possible. A small glass window on the top side allowed the experimenter to view the wing models as they were hit by the wind. Approximately 150 miniature wings, most made out of steel sheets, were tested.

The Wrights were digging the facts out of the speculation again ... and they were happy.

Two Years To Flight: 1902

In early 1902, the organizers of a world's fair which would open in 1904 in St. Louis, Missouri, announced a grand prize of $100,000 for the best manned flight in a flying machine. The Wright brothers were somewhat concerned that some new experimenter would be motivated to make use of their hard-earned discoveries, but they knew they were now on the cutting edge of the field and didn't really expect anyone else to outdo them. The money held no interest for them, since they felt a mercenary motivation would interfere with their research. As it turned out, it was just as well that they didn't enter the contest, because by 1904 the fair was steeped in debt and didn't have any prize money to pay out.

So the brothers spent the winter of 1901 and spring of 1902 working hard on their new glider, without thought of immediate reward. At the same time they had to make their bicycles for the new season, so they could afford to ignore possible prizes. It was a busy time.

Bicycle season came and went. On August 28, Orville and Wilbur were back in Kitty Hawk, anxious to begin a new round of tests. Chanute wanted to join them again, but the brothers really preferred to work on their own and tried to discourage the older man. They would welcome their friend, Chanute's assistant George Spratt, but they felt that the others would slow down their work. In the end, Chanute said he would wait until October before visiting.

The brothers repaired their workshop, damaged by a year of Kitty Hawk's incessant winds, and added a kitchen and living room at the back. They also installed beds above, creating a loft area. This year they planned to be much more comfortable in their camp. The mosquitoes seemed to respect this desire by not showing up to bother them. They brought along a bicycle to shorten the trip time along the sandy road to the town of Kitty Hawk. It used to take them three hours for the round-trip, and now they would make it in just one hour.

On September 8, they began to assemble their new glider. The wings on this one were only slightly larger in square footage, but they were slimmer and longer than before, 32 feet by 5 feet. The wing had a smaller curve whose high point had been moved back a third of the way from the leading edge. The forward elevator was smaller and shaped like a small wing. A major change on this new glider was the addition of a hip cradle which held the pilot snugly and caused the wings

Dan Tate and Wilbur test the unmanned 1902 glider. LC-W861-40

to warp as needed when he moved his body in an instinctive reaction to wing movement. Also new was a 6-foot vertical double tail, a fixed rudder which the brothers hoped would control the glider in a turn.

On September 19, they were ready to begin the tests of their new craft. Dan Tate helped them carry the glider to Little Hill, the smallest of the three Kill Devil Hills.

The long testing of wing shapes in their wind tunnel back in Dayton proved worthwhile—the craft was gliding beautifully. This year Orville wanted to do much more of the flying than he had the previous two years, but before turning the machine over to him, Wilbur wanted to be as certain as possible that there would be no terrible risks in store.

The next day at Big Hill, after a number of successful glides and a few gentle turns, Wilbur tried a sharper turn. A gust of wind lifted the left wing, and Wilbur, not yet fully accustomed to operating this new glider, reacted incorrectly. The glider went out of control and the right wing struck the ground. "Well digging" is what the brothers called it when one wing scraped the ground. As this craft was much stronger than previous gliders, it survived undamaged. Wilbur was just as fortunate and, after analyzing his pilot errors, was ready to go again.

On the morning of Tuesday, September 23, it was Orville's turn to fly. That afternoon one of his flights ended in a stall, as the machine crashed fifty feet to the ground. Incredibly, though the aircraft was badly damaged, Orville wasn't hurt at all. The forward elevator had again saved a life.

Their first visitor in the shed that fall was a mouse that prowled around the kitchen each night looking for a meal. Orville set a trap with food, but the mouse was too clever for him. One night, Orville woke up as the mouse crawled over his face, so he got up to check the trap. In his diary on September 27, Orville wrote, "I found on getting up that the little fellow had only come to tell me to put another piece of corn bread in the trap. He had disposed of the first piece. I have sworn 'vengeance' on the little fellow for this impudence and insult."

The 1902 glider soars with Wilbur as the pilot. LC-W861-183A

On September 30, Lorin Wright arrived, to see what his younger brothers were actually doing in North Carolina. George Spratt came the following day. The glider had been easily repaired after Orville's crash, so both men were able to observe and assist in the tests.

The big problem of 1902 turned out to be an uncontrollable spin, later called a "tailspin," that the craft would go into whenever a sharp turn with steep banking of the wings was attempted. On October 3, after days of intense discussion, Orville came up with the idea that the two fixed vertical rudders in the back were the cause of the spin. He believed that if they had only one rudder and it was movable, the pilot could control the glider during these turns. Wilbur then suggested that the same wires used for wingwarping be attached to the rudder so that the pilot could con-

The moveable single rudder of the 1902 glider allowed the pilot to make sharp turns. LC-W861-7

trol them both at the same time. Since both movements were needed when banking during a turn, with the vertical rudder refining the action of wingwarping's side-to-side control, this made a lot of sense.

On October 5, Octave Chanute and Augustus Herring arrived at Kitty Hawk, bringing one of Chanute's gliders with them. The next day the Wrights' glider's new movable vertical rudder, measuring 5 feet high by 14 inches wide, was finished. On October 8, a series of straight gliding tests was made successfully, with the longest glide measuring 237 feet.

At last, it was possible to control the craft in three dimensions. Pitch, or front-to-back movement, was controlled by the front elevator. Roll, or side-to-side motion, was controlled by wingwarping. Yaw, or turning left or right, was controlled by the rear vertical rudder. With this system, now known as "aileron control," the air pressure on different parts of the machine could be altered to keep the equilibrium. The old idea of shifting body weight was finally put to rest.

On October 13, Lorin left Kitty Hawk and took the good news to Katharine.

For the rest of October the brothers flew hundreds of glides, many with sharp turns, and were tremendously successful. They now had full control of their machine, were able to fly over 650 feet, and could stay in the air for up to 26 seconds on a single flight. They managed to break all previous records for distance, time in the air, and strength of wind overcome. And still, each brother had spent less than two hours total time in the air as pilots.

The 1902 glider in flight with Dan Tate running alongside it. LC-W861-6

Before leaving camp, Orville and Wilbur made the glider more rigid by making the leading edges of the wings immovable. This meant that only the rear outer edges of the wingtips could be warped. They found this "end control" system to work as well as the "full wing" method. The Wrights felt that this design change would work better in an aircraft which needed to withstand the vibrations of a motor—because that would be the next step.

Having made nearly one thousand glides between them, Orville and Wilbur returned to Dayton at the end of October. They were ready for powered flight.

One Year To Flight: 1903

So now the brothers had a glider which was stable and controllable in the air. The next great challenge, then, was to build a power-driven craft which could rise from the ground independent of the earth's forces and continue forward without falling. At the end of 1902, the Wrights, along with the mechanic they'd hired to run the bicycle shop for them, Charlie Taylor, began to design an engine for their "Kitty Hawk Flyer." It had to be small and light enough not to weigh down the craft, yet strong enough to do the required work. Since they weren't able to find one already built, they had to design and build their own. Once they finished the design, Orville and Wilbur concentrated on reworking their aircraft to accommodate the engine, while Charlie went to work on the engine itself.

Six weeks later, the 180 pound, 4 cylinder, 12 horsepower, water-cooled engine was completed. It started with a spark from a dry battery, and, once running, was fed gasoline from a one-gallon tank, which would be attached to an upper wing strut.

The second day the engine was tested, February 13, 1903, the crankcase broke. While Charlie was constructing a new one, Wilbur and Orville turned their attention to propellers.

Propellers would be needed to take the power produced by the engine and turn it into the thrust necessary for forward movement. Although propellers had been used to push water by ships for years, no information existed to tell them how to design a propeller that would push air. The brothers had to come up with their own calculations once again, but were already steps ahead due to their early wind tunnel tests of airfoils. Propeller blades are also airfoils and work as wings do to produce differences in air pressure. An object will move toward lower air pressure (remember that lift is achieved when air pressure above the wing is lower than the pressure below). A turning propeller increases the air pressure behind it, so it moves forward into the area of lower pressure. But as the speed of the forward movement accelerates, the difference in air pressure in front and behind decreases and therefore thrust decreases.

Orville and Wilbur had to figure out how to maintain the thrust needed to keep their plane in the air. They knew that trial and error would waste valuable time. They were determined to come up with a scientific formula using all of the data they could compile to design an effective propeller. Though the equations involved would be daunting for a even trained mathematician, these two self-taught mechanics, working together from their precise observations, succeeded.

They planned to use two rear mounted propellers, connected to the engine by strong, bicycle-type chains, which rotated in opposite directions in order to maintain stability (if they rotated in the same direction, they would tend to turn the machine in that direction). In February 1903, they built and tested a working model of their propeller design. In March, they built two 8½-feet-wide propellers out of spruce, covering the tips with thin canvas to prevent splitting, and finally painted them with aluminum.

During this same time, they made complete drawings of their 1902 glider with its three-dimensional control system and, on March 3, applied for a patent. It would be granted in 1906.

On June 24, Wilbur spoke again to the Western Society of Engineers, presenting the results of their 1902 glider tests. He and Orville had decided to keep their current work with engines and propellers secret. They did not want to be distracted by reporters, nor did they want others using their ideas. They were becoming better known, but until they had the engine-powered machine actually flying, they wanted others to keep away. It was with difficulty that they got Octave Chanute to agree not to visit them in Kitty Hawk at least until late October 1903.

In September the brothers and Charlie Taylor crated everything up for what they hoped would

A well-equipped kitchen, added to the Kitty Hawk workshop in 1902, made the camp much more comfortable. LC-USZ62-65138

be their climactic trip to North Carolina. The whole machine had never been put together in Dayton because the shop was too small. Even with just the middle part assembled, it was impossible to get through their workshop to the front room to see bicycle customers, and they had to go out the side door and in through the front.

On September 23, the Wright brothers again set out, arriving in Kitty Hawk the afternoon of September 25. There was a steady rain and a lot of wind, but they immediately got busy rebuilding their workshop, which had once again been damaged by the severe storms of the previous winter. It had, in fact, been moved two feet off its foundation. Then they turned to constructing a new building to house their *Flyer,* which had not yet arrived.

Fortunately, the 1902 glider was in great shape, and they soon were out practicing piloting over the dunes again. Rediscovering their joy of flight, they glided again and again and again, with one long glide lasting 43 seconds, beating their former record. If there was enough wind they also tried soaring, climbing high into the air while minimizing their forward movement.

On October 3, Orville had a terrifying experience when he was thrown from the pilot's position out onto a wing by a sudden gust of wind. He managed to scramble back to the controls just in time to avoid a crash.

Meanwhile, just over 150 miles to the north, on October 7, Samuel Langley was attempting to launch his newest, 730-pound aerodrome by catapulting it from the top of a houseboat in the Potomac River. Charles Manly, the pilot, was fortunately uninjured as the craft splashed right into the water. Needless to say, the Wright brothers were not displeased that the aerodrome had failed, but they were dismayed when they heard that Langley insisted that the plane would fly once the launch system was corrected. In fact, Langley tried again on December 8—and failed again. Despite his eminent position at the Smithsonian, Langley began to draw a great deal of ridicule from the press, who had become convinced that human flight was a joke. Small wonder the Wrights kept their work mostly under wraps.

Back at Kill Devil Hills, the crates containing the parts of the *Flyer* arrived on October 9, and were immediately followed by several days of pounding rain and fierce winds. Wilbur and Orville were kept busy bracing the new building and repairing its roof. In a letter to Katharine, Wilbur wrote, "The wind and rain continued through the night, but we took the advice of the Oberlin coach, 'Cheer up, boys, there is no hope.' We went to bed, and both slept soundly. In the morning we found the larger part of our floor under water but the kitchen and dining room were all right, the water being merely even with the under side of the floor boards. The front door step was six inches under water. The storm continued through Saturday and Sunday, but by Monday it had reared up so much that it finally fell over on its back and lay quiet." By the time the storm ended the brothers had unpacked the crates and begun work on the *Flyer's* upper wing.

In October, George Spratt joined them at Kitty Hawk. In the days following, more excellent glides in the 1902 craft were made, the best of which was Orville's record-breaking glide on October 26 of 1 minute 11.8 seconds.

Because the weather was quite cold and rainy, a heating system was needed. The brothers built a fire inside a large can which had been placed in the building. Everything was terribly smoky and sooty, so they added a stove pipe for ventilation. Always the inventors!

But Wilbur and Orville were feeling the pressure of the race to see who would have the first successful aeroplane. To Spratt's dismay, they decided to forego testing their new machine as a glider and planned to quickly get it ready for a powered flight.

On November 5, while the engine was being tested, its not-quite-regular firing began jerking the chains leading to the propeller drive shafts, which yanked loose sprockets attached to the shafts and damaged them. Lacking the facilities to fix the shafts meant they had to be sent back to Charlie Taylor in Dayton. Since Spratt was just leaving, he was able to send the shafts via rail express from Norfolk.

From November 7 through 12, Octave Chanute visited them at Kitty Hawk. It was cold, there was little food, and the plane wasn't ready to fly, so Chanute left sooner than expected. In their heart of hearts, Orville and Wilbur were pleased to be alone again.

The brothers remained enthusiastic about their new machine, but were also worried that the engine would not be powerful enough to propel the plane, which with the pilot weighed close to 750 pounds. This new aeroplane was not symmetrical as the gliders had been. The engine was placed on the bottom wing just to the right of center. In the event of a crash, the pilot would at least not have to worry about the engine falling on top of him. To help compensate for this weight, the pilot was positioned to the left of center, and the right wing was four inches longer than the left to provide extra lift for the heavier side.

The total wingspan was 40 feet, 4 inches, and the wing from front to back was 6 feet, 6 inches. The total area of the top and bottom wings was 510 square feet. The wings curved down so the tips were ten inches below the central section, to minimize the effect of wind gusts. They were made with spars of spruce and ribs of ash, covered with unbleached muslin cloth. The *Flyer's* length from nose to tail was 21 feet, 1 inch. Though perhaps wheels would have been easier, the landing gear consisted of two skids braced to the upper and lower wings.

This machine had two movable rear rudders which were connected to the wingwarping controls. There was no complex instrument panel as there is on modern airplanes. Instead there was an anemometer to record wind velocity and the exact distance flown, a stopwatch to record the time of the flight and allow speed calculation, and an instrument to record the number of propeller turns.

While waiting for the return of the repaired drive shafts, Orville and Wilbur prepared and tested their launching rail system. For takeoff, the aircraft's runners rested on a plank which was placed across a trolley. The trolley was made of a wooden block riding on two wheel hubs adapted from a bicycle. There was also a third cycle hub which was attached to a smaller plank placed between the front part of the runners, to prevent the nose of the craft from falling. The trolley then rolled along a "monorail." The track and trolley had only cost them $4, compared to the $50,000 spent by Langley for his (non-functional) launch system.

The night of November 17 was freezing cold, and Wilbur wrote home with this description: "In addition to . . . 1, 2, 3, and 4 blankets, we now have 5 blanket nights, & 5 blankets & 2 quilts. Next comes 5 blankets, 2 quilts & fire; then 5, 2, fire, & hot-water jug. This is as far as we have got so far. Next comes the addition of sleeping without undressing, then shoes & hats, and finally overcoats. We intend to be comfortable while we are here."

On November 20, the rebuilt propeller drive shafts arrived. The brothers quickly reattached them, but the engine still jerked too much and there was danger of the sprockets coming loose again. This time they froze the connections with an extremely strong cement glue and the problem was solved.

On November 28, after several days of wind, rain, and even snow, they ran the engine a few times to test its power before actually flying with it. It worked wonderfully and they no longer worried about having enough power to sustain a flight. However, the strain on the propeller shafts, while not loosening the sprockets, caused a crack to appear in one of the shafts, and they could not risk a flight with it.

The brothers realized that they needed steel shafts instead of wood, and the only way to get them was to go back to Dayton to make them.

Despite the worsening weather, they were determined to test their aeroplane before the year was finished. Orville immediately left for Dayton while Wilbur stayed behind.

By December 11, Orville had returned with the new steel propeller shafts, and the next day the *Kitty Hawk Flyer* was ready to be tested. There was very little wind that day, making takeoff more difficult, but they wanted to go ahead. Before the launch, however, they accidentally broke the point of the rudder, and it took another two days to get ready to try again.

Finally, on December 14, at 1:30 P.M., a flag hung from the workshed signaled to the men of the Kill Devil Hill Lifesaving Station a mile away that the Wright brothers were about to begin the

The 1903 flyer, complete with engine, at rest beside the camp at Kitty Hawk. LC-W861-16

Local witnesses stand before the Wright Brothers and their 1903 flyer, on its track and ready for launch, December 14, 1903. LC-USZ62-56774

first test of an engine-powered aeroplane. If the brothers flew, they wanted to be sure that it could be proven. Arriving to witness this historic event were five men, two little boys, and their dog.

The *Flyer* was wheeled along the "Junction Railroad," the movable track which made carrying the heavy machine unnecessary, to the launch site a quarter of a mile away. When the plane was in position, the engine was started and the propellers began to spin. Wilbur won the coin toss and climbed into the pilot's position.

There were supports placed under the wingtips to steady the craft while it was stationary. When ready for takeoff, the supports were removed and two men held the wingtips as the engine began to run. Then they let go as Wilbur flipped the clip to release the restraining rope. The rope did not release; it was too tight. So a few of the men helped push the machine back up the rail a few inches, to loosen the rope enough to slip the *Flyer* free.

The craft started to move along the monorail and down the gentle slope of the dune. The wind was very light that afternoon so the plane's speed as it took off was a little bit slow. Wilbur mistakenly turned the plane up too sharply as it left the track, causing it to slow even more. There was no time to correct the error and the aircraft sank to the ground, breaking some of the front rudder supports. But the brothers were encouraged, because the repairs would be easy and Wilbur had figured out what he had done wrong.

For the next couple of days the winds were first too slow and then too fast, and the brothers worried that conditions might be poor until the next spring. They couldn't tolerate the idea of waiting, so despite strong winds, they prepared for another test on Thursday, December 17. This time they laid the track on the flat beach near the shed.

Responding to the signal flag on this day were John Daniels, Will Dough, Adam Etheridge, W. C. Brinkley, and Johnny Moore, a teenager who had been visiting the Kill Devil Hill lifesaving station. Watching through a spyglass from the station was Bob Wescott, and watching from the Kitty Hawk Station through his telescope was

Orville Wright making the world's first free, controlled, and sustained flight in a heavier-than-air, power-driven aeroplane, on December 17, 1903. LC-W861-35

Captain S. J. Payne. John Daniels was assigned to take a photograph of the aeroplane as it left the track, using a camera which Orville had set on a tripod and carefully aimed.

Now it was Orville's turn to man the aircraft. Daniels said later, "After a while they shook hands, and we couldn't help notice how they held on to each other's hand, sort o' like they hated to let go; like two folks parting who weren't sure they'd ever see each other again."

Orville climbed into the *Flyer*. He started along the launching rails at 10:35 A.M. as the onlookers loudly cheered him on. Wilbur ran alongside holding onto the bottom wing. The aeroplane took off and flew for twelve seconds.

One thousand one,
One thousand two,
One thousand three,
One thousand four,
One thousand five,
One thousand six,
One thousand seven,
One thousand eight,
One thousand nine,
One thousand ten,
One thousand eleven,
One thousand twelve.
Orville landed 120 feet away.
Man had flown.

Afterword

Just like Wilbur a few days before, Orville had difficulty with the front elevator, which could too easily be overcontrolled. They would both take great care with this in the next few trials.

The men carried the plane back to the launch site, and Wilbur prepared for the next trial. The wind had slowed down a little, so Wilbur was able to go a little farther before descending.

On Orville's next ride a gust of wind and a wrong move by the pilot caused the plane to go down and the left wing to hit the ground. Fortunately the craft was not damaged, and at noon Wilbur again climbed into the machine.

The strong gusts of wind buffeted the aircraft for the first 300 feet of flight, but then Wilbur improved his control and managed the winds fine until one great gust took the plane down. The land distance traveled was 852 feet and the flight had lasted 59 seconds. Taking the wind speed and other factors into consideration, the air distance measured over half a mile. The *Kitty Hawk Flyer* was an indisputable success!

The four flights of the day ended with no question that Orville and Wilbur Wright had achieved their goal of flying a plane which lifted into the air by its own power, continued forward without slowing down, and landed at a point no lower than its launching point, all the while under the control of a pilot.

A telegram, partially garbled in transmission, was sent to their father, Bishop Wright. "Success four flights Thursday morning all against twenty one mile wind started from Level with engine power alone average speed through air thirty one miles longest 57 [actually 59] seconds inform Press home #### Christmas. Orevelle [Orville] Wright."

The newspaper reports describing the event were confused and incorrect. The brothers did not trust the newspapers, giving them very little information and no photographs. Concerned that others would use their ideas before a patent could be awarded, they became very secretive about their designs. So their achievement garnered little attention, and few people understood the great advance made on December 17, 1903.

The brothers moved their operations back to the Dayton area and began the mechanical work of expanding upon their success. In 1905, Wilbur stayed up 38 minutes and flew more than 24 miles. In 1908, Orville flew with a passenger for over an hour. In that year, they signed commercial agreements with the United States and France to manufacture aeroplanes. Finally, the Wright brothers were acclaimed internationally.

But with acclaim came lawyers. Other inventors began infringing on the Wright brothers' patents, and instead of devoting their energies toward further research, they were diverted into lawsuits. Augustus Herring, Chanute's assistant, wrote that he, in fact, had invented the aeroplane, and offered to form a company with the Wrights as his partners. Wilbur, always the most eloquent of the brothers, spent more and more time in court, and it wore him down. In the spring of 1912 he fell victim to typhoid fever, the same disease that had almost killed his brother, and he died on May 30, 1912, at age 45.

In 1915, Orville sold the Wright Company for more than a million dollars and went back to pure research. He lived to be 76, and died in Dayton, Ohio, on January 21, 1948.

From 1928 through 1948, the *Kitty Hawk Flyer* was exhibited at the Science Museum in South Kensington, London. It was then installed at the Smithsonian Institution in Washington, D.C. on December 17, 1948, 45 years after its historic first flight.

On July 20, 1969, 65 years after that flight, a piece of wing fabric from the *Flyer* was carried by astronaut Neil Armstrong, when he became the first man to walk on the surface of the moon.

"We knew that men had by common consent adopted human flight as the standard of impossibility. When a man said, 'It can't be done; a man might as well try to fly,' he was understood as expressing the final limit of impossibility. Our own growing belief that man might nevertheless learn to fly was based on the idea that while thousands of creatures of the most dissimilar bodily structures, such as insects, fishes, reptiles, birds, and mammals, were flying every day at pleasure, it was reasonable to suppose that men might also fly. . . ."

—Wilbur Wright,
just before his death in 1912

TREASURE TROVES OF FACT-FILLED FUN FROM AVON CAMELOT

HOW TO TRAVEL THROUGH TIME
by James M. Deem   76681-7/ $3.50 US/ $4.50 CAN

HOW TO CATCH A FLYING SAUCER
by James M. Deem   71898-7/ $3.50 US/ $4.50 CAN

HOW TO HUNT BURIED TREASURE
by James M. Deem   72176-7/ $3.99 US/ $4.99 CAN

ASK ME ANYTHING ABOUT THE PRESIDENTS
by Louis Phillips   76426-1/ $3.99 US/ $4.99 CAN

ASK ME ANYTHING ABOUT BASEBALL
by Louis Phillips   78029-1/ $3.99 US/ $4.99 CAN

EXPLORING AUTUMN
by Sandra Markle   71910-X/ $3.50 US/ $4.50 CAN

GOBBLE! THE COMPLETE BOOK OF THANKSGIVING WORDS
by Lynda Graham-Barber   71963-0/ $3.99 US/ $4.99 CAN

Buy these books at your local bookstore or use this coupon for ordering:

Mail to: Avon Books, Dept BP, Box 767, Rte 2, Dresden, TN 38225   D
Please send me the book(s) I have checked above.
❑ My check or money order—no cash or CODs please—for $_____ is enclosed (please add $1.50 to cover postage and handling for each book ordered—Canadian residents add 7% GST).
❑ Charge my VISA/MC Acct#_____ Exp Date_____
Minimum credit card order is two books or $7.50 (please add postage and handling charge of $1.50 per book—Canadian residents add 7% GST). For faster service, call 1-800-762-0779. Residents of Tennessee, please call 1-800-633-1607. Prices and numbers are subject to change without notice. Please allow six to eight weeks for delivery.

Name_____
Address_____
City_____ State/Zip_____
Telephone No._____   CNF 0595

*Eighty-two tricks you **can't** do!*

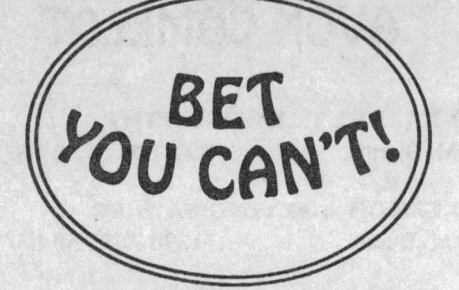

BET YOU CAN'T!

Science Impossibilities to Fool You
by Vicki Cobb and Kathy Darling
illus. by Martha Weston
Avon Camelot 0-380-54502-0/$3.99/$4.99

Bet you can't tear a piece of paper into three equal parts, or make two pencil tips meet. Bet you can't blow up a balloon in a bottle. Bet you can't keep a match burning over a glass of soda. Here are over seventy deceptively simple—and impossible—feats to stump friends and family while introducing the scientific principles of gravity, mechanics, logic, and perception. Winner of the Academy of Science Children's Book Award.

Also by Vicki Cobb and Kathy Darling
BET YOU CAN! *Science Possibilities to Fool You*
82180-X • **$3.99** U.S. $4.99 CAN

Buy these books at your local bookstore or use this coupon for ordering:

Mail to: Avon Books, Dept BP, Box 767, Rte 2, Dresden, TN 38225   D
Please send me the book(s) I have checked above.
❏ My check or money order—no cash or CODs please—for $_____ is enclosed (please add $1.50 to cover postage and handling for each book ordered—Canadian residents add 7% GST).
❏ Charge my VISA/MC Acct#_____ Exp Date_____
Minimum credit card order is two books or $7.50 (please add postage and handling charge of $1.50 per book—Canadian residents add 7% GST). For faster service, call 1-800-762-0779. Residents of Tennessee, please call 1-800-633-1607. Prices and numbers are subject to change without notice. Please allow six to eight weeks for delivery.

Name_____
Address_____
City_____State/Zip_____
Telephone No._____
BNO 0595